Race Further with Reading

THE AWFUL
ASTRONAUT

By Damian Harvey

Illustrated by Davide Ortu

W

CHAPTER 1
A Dream Come True

Sam was about to take a huge mouthful of Astro-Pops Space Crispies when the twins burst into the kitchen.

"There's a letter for you Dad," cried Tom.

"And there's a rocket on the envelope!" added Tim, waving it above his head.

Sam dropped his spoon and forgot all about breakfast. Milk and cereal splashed everywhere.

"I've been waiting for this," he said.

"Open it!" said Mrs Jones.

"But what if I'm not going?" asked Sam.

"There's only one way to find out," replied his wife.

"OPEN IT!" cried Tom and Tim, excitedly.

Sam slowly opened the envelope and read the letter.

"I've been chosen!" he cried. "I'm going into space!"

For as long as he could remember, Sam Jones had wanted to be an astronaut. When he was little he had talked about nothing but rockets and outer space. In bed he dreamed of flying across the stars on a mission to explore strange new worlds.

His room had been full of space stuff. Posters covered the walls and model rockets hung from the ceiling. He even had plastic planets that lit up, and glow-in-the-dark stars. Everyone thought he would grow out of it – but he never did.

As he grew up, Sam thought more and more about becoming an astronaut. Then one day, he spotted something in the newspaper.

"This is my chance," thought Sam.

A few months later, Sam was given the job. He could hardly believe it! But becoming an astronaut wasn't easy.

Sam had spent six years training with the other astronauts. First they spent a week living underground in deep, dark caves. "These tunnels are very small!" complained Sam.

"This is how it will feel living on the Space Station," said Commander Klopp.

Then they had to sleep in frozen forests in the middle of Russia.

"I'm f-f-freezing!" shivered Sam.

"It's c-c-colder than this in space," said Commander Klopp. Sam thought things couldn't get any worse, but he was wrong.

Next they had to wear a spacesuit and move around under water.

"I can't swim!" gasped Sam.

"This is how it feels when you walk in space," said Kasper.

But worst of all, they had to sit in a little pod as it whizzed round and round.

"I feel dizzy!" sobbed Sam.

"This is how it will feel when the rocket takes off," laughed Commander Klopp.

CHAPTER 2
How to be an Astronaut

The twins could hardly wait to tell their school friends the news.

"I don't believe you," said Megan. "Your dad's not an astronaut."

"Yeah!" laughed Kyle. "Only cool people can be astronauts."

"Dad says anyone can be an astronaut," said Tom. "If they really want to be."

"But your dad's too clumsy," said Zack.

"That's true," thought Tim.

Dad was always tripping over or bumping into things. He was probably the clumsiest person on Earth. Soon he would be the clumsiest person in space, too.

When the teacher came in, she let the twins show everyone what their dad did. "He had to learn survival skills," said Tim. "This is him camping in the snow." "And this is when he fell into an icy river," added Tom. Everyone laughed.

"Then he got chased by a huge bear," said Tom, showing them another picture.

The whole class gasped with surprise. "Here's Dad trying on his spacesuit," said Tom. "Cool!" everyone agreed.

When the day of the launch arrived, Tom, Tim, and their whole family were there to watch. Their friends at school watched it on the television – and so did millions of other people around the world.

In the command module, the three astronauts prepared for lift-off.

"It feels like I've forgotten something," said Sam. The rocket's huge engines roared into life and Sam felt his seat shaking.

"Oh dear," he said. "Now I remember – I get travel sick!"

Commander Klopp opened her mouth to speak, but a loud voice said "LIFT-OFF!"

Sam felt himself being pushed down into his seat as the rocket took to the skies. Faster and faster, higher and higher it went.

"Help!" yelled Sam. "I want to get off!"

CHAPTER 3
Astro-Pops

After they had left the Earth's atmosphere,

Sam started to enjoy the journey.

"Space is awesome," he said, looking out

at the stars.

"There's the space station," said Kasper.

"That was quick," said Sam. "How fast are we going?"

"Over 17,000 miles an hour," smiled Kasper.

Sam groaned and closed his eyes.

"I don't even like fast rollercoasters," he said. He didn't open his eyes again until they were safely on the space station.

Sam's locker was small. He was having trouble getting everything to fit, especially the box the twins had given him.

"I wonder what's inside?" he thought, giving it a shake. Suddenly the lid popped off and Astro-Pops Space Crispies flew into the air!

"Come back!" cried Sam. But the Astro-Pops didn't listen. They drifted across the space station like a silent swarm of bees. "The commander won't like this," said Kasper.

"Doesn't she like Astro-Pops?" asked Sam.

"Yes, but she hates mess," said Kasper. "And if we don't catch them there could be a disaster."

"Yes," agreed Sam. "No Astro-Pops for breakfast."

"There's only one thing we can do," said
Sam. "We will have to eat them all."
The two astronauts floated around like
giant goldfish, scooping up cereal in their
mouths.

"There's too many," said Sam, swallowing another mouthful.

"They are too dry," complained Kasper.

Sam had just the thing. "Milk!" he said and poured a drop onto some passing Crispies.

"NO!" cried Kasper. But it was too late …

The milk was already floating around like a lump of jelly.

"Now we'll have to catch that too," said Kasper. Just then, Commander Klopp came in. "What in the galaxy is going on?" she demanded.

Before anyone could answer, Klopp grabbed a box with a long tube on the end. Then she pressed a button and the flying Crispies started disappearing into it.

"What about the milk?" asked Sam.

Klopp took a thin tube from her pocket and stuck it into the floating milk.

"Delicious!" she slurped. "Now get ready."

"What for?" asked Sam.

"A space walk," said Klopp.

CHAPTER 4
Space Walk

Sam could hardly wait to go on a space

walk, but getting their suits on was tricky.

"It's very dark," said Sam, peering through

the window. Commander Klopp sighed.

"Your helmet's on the wrong way round."

Finally, the three astronauts picked up their equipment bags and stepped into the airlock. The door closed behind them with a clang.

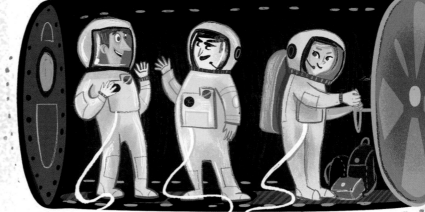

"Fasten your safety lines," came Klopp's voice in their helmets. "We don't want you drifting away." Sam gave a thumbs up and the outer door slowly opened.

"I'm stepping through the hatch," said Kasper.

Sam watched as Kasper floated outside.

His bags floated behind him.

"Me next!" he thought, his heart beating with excitement. But as Sam took a step forward he tripped over the edge of the hatch. "Oops!" he cried, diving head first in slow motion.

29

"Stop messing about," said Kasper, holding Sam's arm. "We have work to do."

Outside the space station, Sam made sure everything was fastened to a handrail. He didn't want anything to float away.

Looking around, Sam could see lots of stars but the darkness of space was bigger than he had imagined. Below them, Earth looked like a giant ball. He saw clouds moving over the land and seas. He could even see city lights glowing in the night.

"It looks so beautiful!" said Sam.

But a space walk wasn't all fun. They worked for hours fitting wires and doing repairs. "This is boring," complained Sam, snipping pieces of wire with his cutters. Suddenly one of Kasper's tool bags started drifting away … and now, so was Kasper.

"What's happening?" Kasper cried.

Sam spotted Kasper's safety line floating

behind him like a snake.

"Oh no!" he said. "I must have cut

that while I was snipping the wires."

"Do something!" Kasper yelled.

...ea popped into Sam's head. He quickly grabbed the equipment bags and fastened them together like a string of sausages. Then Sam pushed himself from the space station. "Here I come," he shouted.

Sam floated slowly through space towards the other astronaut. He just managed to grab the end of Kasper's safety line. "That was close," said Sam, pulling them both back to safety.

CHAPTER 5
Back to Earth

After the space walk there were lots of other jobs to do.

"First you can clean the sleeping pods," said Commander Klopp. "That should keep you out of trouble."

Sam nodded sadly. He was trying to be a great astronaut but somehow things kept going wrong.

"Everything needs packing into the capsule," said Kasper.

"I can do that," said Sam.

"You've been working hard," said Commander Klopp. "Well done."

Sam grinned. "Perhaps I'm not such an awful astronaut after all," he thought.

"Time for a nap," yawned Sam. "Before I get another job to do." Instead of going to his sleeping pod, Sam stretched himself out in the capsule. As he slept, he didn't notice his foot bump against the door or his hands touching the controls.

When Sam woke up, Commander Klopp's voice was shouting from the screen. "Sam!" she yelled. "What have you done?"

"I've packed everything," Sam replied proudly.

"You have launched the capsule," Commander Klopp yelled.

"And we're not in it," added Kasper.

Sam could hardly believe his ears. He looked through the window and stared. The space station was nowhere to be seen.

For one moment, Sam knew exactly what to do. He put on his spacesuit, climbed into his seat and fastened the seatbelt.

"Now what?" he thought.

The capsule rattled and shook as it went faster and faster. Sam was starting to feel strange. His whole body was feeling very heavy.

"What's happening?" he asked.

A new voice came through the speakers in Sam's helmet.

"This is ground control," said the voice.

"You're coming home Sam."

"But I don't know what to do!" he cried, starting to panic.

"Just hold tight," said the voice.

Outside, Sam heard the sound of rushing
wind as the capsule fell to Earth,
spinning as it went.

"It's like being on a fairground ride,"
thought Sam.

Suddenly there was a huge jolt as the capsule's parachute opened. Sam was just starting to relax when there was a heavy thud. It felt like the capsule had been hit by an enormous truck.

Everything was quiet. Then the capsule's door opened.

"Welcome home Sam," said a friendly voice.

"That was awesome!" cried Sam with a big grin. "Can I do it again?"

Franklin Watts
First published in Great Britain in 2016 by
The Watts Publishing Group

Text © Damian Harvey 2016
Illustrations © Davide Ortu 2016

The rights of Damian Harvey to be
identified as the author and Davide Ortu
as the illustrator of this Work have been
asserted in accordance with the Copyright,
Designs and Patents Act, 1988.

Series Editor: Melanie Palmer
Series Advisor: Catherine Glavina
Cover Designer: Cathryn Gilbert
Design Manager: Peter Scoulding

A CIP catalogue record for this book is
available from the British Library.

ISBN 978 1 4451 4988 2 (hbk)
ISBN 978 1 4451 4990 5 (pbk)
ISBN 978 1 4451 4989 9 (library ebook)

Printed in China

Franklin Watts
An imprint of
Hachette Children's Group
Part of The Watts Publishing Group
Carmelite House
50 Victoria Embankment
London EC4Y 0DZ

An Hachette UK Company
www.hachette.co.uk

www.franklinwatts.co.uk

FSC
www.fsc.org

MIX
Paper from
responsible sources
FSC® C104740